MW01130244

Dear Claire,

Read books and journey through new imaginative experiences. We hope you will always have a fondness for reading books. May your life be filled with diverse friendships.

Best wishes,
Beverly Samuel
Alyssa Samuel

Make New Friends

SCHOOL

BY BEVERLY SAMUEL & ALYSSA SAMUEL

iUniverse books may be ordered through booksellers or by contacting:

iUniverse
1663 Liberty Drive
Bloomington, IN 47403
www.iuniverse.com
844-349-9409

Because of the dynamic nature of the Internet, any web addresses or links contained in this book may have changed since publication and may no longer be valid. The views expressed in this work are solely those of the author and do not necessarily reflect the views of the publisher, and the publisher hereby disclaims any responsibility for them.

ISBN: 978-1-6632-3274-8 (sc)
ISBN: 978-1-6632-3285-4 (hc)
ISBN: 978-1-6632-3275-5 (e)

Library of Congress Control Number: 2021924534

Print information available on the last page.

iUniverse revised date: 01/22/2022

Beverly Samuel and her daughter, Alyssa, share a story about diversity, equity, and inclusion. This book, dedicated to David Ryan, was inspired by their family's experiences in school, work, and the community.

Skipping happily into the classroom, I said hello to my teacher.
I was so excited about my first day at a brand-new school.
I looked around and saw a colorful poster that read,
"Treat others as you want to be treated: The Golden Rule."

I remembered what my parents taught me.
"Everyone is different. Don't be shy, and have no fear.
Make new friends this school year."

Welcome Students!

I searched for my name tag to find my desk.
My teacher instructed us to introduce ourselves to our group.
I smiled and said, "Hi, I'm Ava.
A fun fact about me is my favorite food is chicken noodle soup."

I looked around the classroom and did not see any familiar faces.
No one was the same. Some had braids, straight, or curly hair.
Some were taller or shorter and had a rainbow of skin colors.
I wanted to make new friends, so we could play, laugh, and share.

"Everyone is different. Don't be shy, and have no fear.
Make new friends this school year."

My teacher explained all the fun things we would learn this year.
After lunch and recess, the day quickly came to an end.
I told my parents all about my first day at school.
And they said, "Be nice and kind; tomorrow you will make new friends.

The next morning at school, I sat at my desk and waited for the lesson.
A girl walked over and sat in her chair.
I said, "Your hair is so pretty! What is your name?"
She replied, "Thanks! My name is Imani, and my mother did my hair."

I asked, "Can your mother fix my hair that way?"
She giggled and said, "Yes, I will ask her tonight."
At recess, Imani and I played together on the slide and swings.
My favorite part was picking flowers in the sunlight.

As I picked daisies, there was a girl in the field with a beautiful dress.
The dress had purple and gold colors that were so bright.
I asked her, "What is your name?" She said, "Priya."
I jokingly asked her if I could have her dress, since we were the same height.

She laughed and said, "Maybe, when I'm done wearing it."
I asked, "Do you like flowers, just like me?"
Priya said, "Roses, tulips, sunflowers, and more.
We can pick flowers together through May, you see."

"Everyone is different. Don't be shy, and have no fear.
Make new friends this school year."

Imani and Priya were my new friends, and we had much in common.
I was so hungry and couldn't wait to eat lunch.
I sat at the table with my new friends.
A boy was eating something different with a crunch.

I asked him, "What are you eating?"
He replied, "Rice crackers as a snack.
They are from the country where I was born, China.
My family and I travel there sometimes to go back."

I said, "Those look so delicious! What is your name?"
He said, "Chao," with a friendly grin.
"I enjoy trying different foods at restaurants all the time."
I said, "Let me tell you about some foods I've tasted. Where do I begin?"

Imani, Priya, Chao, Jamal, and I laughed and talked the entire lunch.
Then it was time for art class to start.
I'm creative and enjoy coloring and painting.
This class would be my favorite part!

"Everyone is different. Don't be shy, and have no fear.
Make new friends this school year."

13

The teacher said we could draw our favorite animal.
I couldn't decide between cats or dogs for my drawing.
So I asked the girl next to me which animal I should choose.
She replied, "*Perros*, of course—cats are always pawing."

GET CREATIVE

I asked, "What does *perros* mean?"
She replied, "It means 'dogs' in my first language, Spanish.
I speak Spanish at home with my family.
I have no friends to speak with me at school—I only wish."

I said, "I can learn Spanish, and we can be friends.
I want to learn new words each day. What is your name?"
She responded, "Rosa, after my *abuela*—my grandmother."
"That's beautiful! I was named after my grandmother, so we are the same."

"Everyone is different. Don't be shy, and have no fear.
Make new friends this school year."

GET CREATIVE

Rosa talked about how she loved to paint and sketch.
She taught me how to say cat, or *gato*.
I couldn't wait to be able to speak Spanish well.
I even learned how to say fish, or *pescado*.

My school day was finally over, so I ran to my bus.
I sat in an empty seat next to a boy with a ball.
He had a small hat on his head.
I asked, "Why is your hat so small?"

He explained, "It is a yarmulke.
My name is David, and I am a Jew."
I said, "That's amazing! I am a Christian."
He said, "I only eat kosher foods; it is part of our religious view."

"Everyone is different. Don't be shy, and have no fear.
Make new friends this school year."

I was excited to tell my parents about school.
I thought about all the new friends I made each day.
This was the best school year ever!
I planned a fun party for my birthday.

My parents said to limit my birthday list to three people.
I smiled and remembered the poster I saw at school.
I invited all my new friends!
"Treat others as you want to be treated: The Golden Rule."

I was happy to have my new friends at my birthday party.
We ate cake, ice cream, and played games at the park.
It was my favorite party, with everyone invited.
We roasted marshmallows after dark.

My new friends taught me more about myself.
I learned so much that was new to me.
We have so many things in common.
Friends are fun. Do you agree?

"Everyone is different. Don't be shy, and have no fear.
Make new friends this school year."

Printed in the United States
by Baker & Taylor Publisher Services